THE CHRISTMAS PICKUP

ABBY KNOX

The book is dedicated to the random nice dude who once picked up my stubborn ass in a blizzard at night. I still can't drive worth a damn in snow.

Merry Christmas!

THE CHRISTMAS PICKUP

BY ABBY KNOX

Tow truck driver Bear Bailey is the city's unsung hero on Christmas Eve, out rescuing stranded motorists in the decade's worst snowstorm. When he happens to spot the cute local weather girl stuck on the side of the road, his Christmas wish has just come true. He'll be picking her up, but has no plans to drop her off anytime soon.

Meteorologist Mary Reed knows all too well she shouldn't be out driving in weather like this. But she has very good reasons. Her car ends up in a snow drift, because of course it does, and it seems like her Christmas Eve plans might be a bust. Out of nowhere, a hot and possessive tow truck driver rolls up and snatches her out of the blizzard. Plans? What plans?

The connection is instant, but there's only one problem: there's lots of other people out there in need of help before Bear can get a taste of Mary's "Christmas cookies!"

WARNING: This book is short, sweet, smutty and full of as much toasty-warm goodness as you can stand. This is full of snowstorm shenanigans with a quirky cast of characters alongside the a kind-hearted, possessive alpha and the sassy heroine. A happily ever after and a Merry Christmas guaranteed!

CHAPTER 1

Bear

Heavy snow is blanketing my driveway tonight, and the wind is just beginning to pick up and whip all the white stuff into a frenzy.

Pretty soon, the drifts will swoop halfway up my front steps and the street will be invisible.

But it's all child's play to the monstrosity parked out front. The only tires bigger than those on my tow truck belong on a tractor. Not to mention the enormous snowplow I added on the front end. There's nothing my sweet Snow Angel can't plow through. Yeah, it's a sissy nickname for a tow truck, but I dare you to say that to my face.

The small city I live in may appear like a winter wonderland on Christmas Eve. It certainly is that way for everyone who may be tucked snugly into the warm living rooms, next to their Christmas trees and lit fireplaces. But for anyone out there on the roads, it's a nightmare.

I'm watching the news, and it doesn't look good.

The local weather girl is telling me the overnight blizzard is going to create white-out conditions on all major roads tonight. Slick surfaces out on the country roads.

After a while, I'm barely registering what she's saying. So why am I watching this?

The weather she's describing may be ugly, but she is anything but. Sweet gingerbread, is she beautiful.

I've admired her on the television from the comfort of my living room for years.

Our local news station is relatively low key in this small city of about 50,000 people, so they aren't really uptight about the dress code on Christmas Eve night. Tonight she's wearing a fitted red sweater with elves all over it, and dangly wreath earrings. And I notice she's wearing her snowflake scarf. She rotates between that one, a red one with candy canes and a white one with holly berries every winter season. I don't know shit about fashion, but I take notice of everything when it comes to her.

She's also wearing black jeans that are nice and tight. The whole ensemble shows off some sweet curves and she's jutting one hip out as she talks. Her voice feels like my favorite Christmas carol.

"I'm standing outside the Weather Center right now, and as you can see," the indomitable Mary Reed says as she gestures around, "the snow is already falling pretty heavily and the wind gusts are getting stronger by the minute. I advise everyone to stay off the roads if you can. If you're not already at your Christmas Eve destinations, I strongly suggest you stay where you are. It's better to stay safe than to get to that party tonight, folks."

She ought to take her own advice and wear a coat and a hat outside. But I'm not going to complain about the way her sassy little hip owns its space and holds dominion over me while she's smiling for the camera. Sometimes I think she should have been a model. But then she wouldn't live in this city and I'd lose my weather girl. And that would not be acceptable.

Mary Reed's sleek, shoulder-length brown hair, as always, has been hair-sprayed within an inch of its life. I've seen it wild and soft and sexy, falling across my pillow. At least, when I close my eyes at night, I have. When I close my eyes and dream of the perfect woman, it's Mary Reed's hair woven between my fingers. Her dark, silky locks are the only ones I imagine feathering across my abs while her soft, thick lips tease their way down…

But that's a Christmas fantasy. Plenty of eligible bachelors in this city are probably lined up if she's not already taken. Guys with way more money and more interesting jobs than me.

I turn off the TV and lace up my boots. Pull on my stocking cap and gloves and grab my keys.

As soon as Martha, light of my life, hears the jingle of keys, she comes running.

I open the door and she bounds outside. I have to hustle to open the tow truck door for her, and as soon as I do, she launches herself into the cab. Unlike most of my passengers, like my mom, Martha doesn't require the use of the extra-long running boards I had installed.

I drive the few blocks to my mom's house, and even in that span of five minutes, the wind is really starting to blow. Snowbanks are creeping up the sides of houses and buildings. Sidewalks are already covered over with sleek white sheets.

And it's just getting started. Tonight is gonna be a bitch.

Mom opens the door as soon I head up the walk. Martha runs to her. Mom gives Martha a hug even before she puts her arm around her own son's neck. It's OK though, that's the effect Martha has on people.

"Have you eaten? I have soup."

She's always looking out for me. She makes too much food for herself and insists on sharing. Hopefully one day she'll have a bunch of grandkids to focus on instead of trying to fatten me up.

"I'm not coming inside, Ma, I don't wanna get snow everywhere. Besides Mary Reed says we're gonna get pounded tonight, so I'm headed out."

Mom knows me too well and smirks at me. "She's a cute one, that Mary Reed. You should write her a letter!"

"Ma, come on. I'm not a creep."

"It's not creepy! She would love you." Mom pops over to kiss me and I have to bend down so she can reach my forehead. Then she taps me on the cheek. "Who wouldn't love this face?"

"Any woman in her right mind?"

"Don't say such things about my son. You be careful tonight."

"Always am, Ma. Thanks for taking Martha."

I say goodbye to my mom, telling her I'll be back tomorrow for Christmas lunch with her and Martha.

Tonight, I've got other things on my mind than women.

CHAPTER 2

Mary

"Merry Christmas, fellas," I say as the last of the news crew files out the door. I've got a giant red sack full of presents and I'm wearing my favorite green sequined elf hat. I have twelve more hats like this at home, some with faux fur, some bedazzled. I may have an addiction to these things.

I've been the chief meteorologist for our middle-market TV station for the past several years, and this is my favorite night of the year to work.

Christmas Eve.

Nothing makes me happier than signing off the nightly news with the annual Santa's sleigh radar update. I get a huge kick out of picturing thousands of parents trundling their little kids off to bed, citing my radar report.

What I love even more than adding to the Christmas spirit on TV is handing out gifts to the crew.

Because my face is on TV and social media, I receive

more gifts from strangers than I care to admit. You would not believe the cards, letters, flowers and sweet messages that show up to the station every day for the anchors and for me, even at a relatively small station such as ours.

But no viewers ever has a care for the people behind the camera. Not to brag, but I've taken it upon myself to make that my job.

Every year, I go out and buy a few little things—coffee shop gift cards, woolen socks, hand warmers, coffee mugs—OK, fine, I go completely overboard—and pass them out to everyone working at the station on Christmas Eve.

I'm not telling you this to make you think I'm such a generous person. I'm telling you this so you understand why I don't get an early enough start on the roads this evening. So you understand how I find myself driving in a snowstorm—against my own advice—trying to get to my friend Jenna's Christmas Eve party.

Jenna is my boss, our news editor, and also happens to be my best friend. She's about ten years older than me but has been like a mother to me ever since my mom and dad passed away in a car wreck when I was fresh out of school.

Jenna gave me my first job as a reporter and helped convince the corporate media bigwigs at our parent company to fund my meteorology and atmospheric sciences studies at night.

Jenna took today off from work to get ready for the holiday and even offered to have me over for Christmas Eve tonight. I told her I would think about it. I'm half tempted to hole up in my house with *It's a Wonderful Life* and some Chinese takeout. It's not that I'm antisocial. I love Jenna's parties. But as I get older, the harder it is to go to holiday parties alone. I'm a bit of an old soul who believes in love at first sight. My parents and grandparents both told me stories about how they knew the moment they met their true loves. They were of a generation that wasted no time.

As yet, there simply has not been any man who's flipped that switch in me.

So, watching George Bailey and Mary Hatch fall in love in black and white is my Christmas Eve jam in recent years.

Tonight though, I just have this feeling that I'll never meet my George Bailey — pillar of the community, hard worker, believer in the little guy, passionate husband and sweet father — if I stay home with my Chinese takeout.

The rest of the crew take off in their SUVs and pickups outfitted with snow tires. I start up my Toyota. It's nothing fancy, but it's never broken down on me yet. I should have invested in snow tires. I usually wait until January to put on those things. We don't have a ton of snow at Christmas. The worst of the storms come after December.

But nature did not wait for my plans this year.

The storm is starting to freak me out a bit and crave some company. And if I'm snowed in, I'd much rather not be alone. There's another very good reason to go to Jenna's.

That's enough of a sign for me.

Well, there's only one thing to do. I phone Jenna as I point my car in the direction of her house.

"Babe!" she cries. "Are you coming? Oh gosh, I'm so glad you're not going to be stuck in your house alone with General Tso and suicidal George Bailey tonight. We need you here! We've got a seat by the fire waiting just for you."

I laugh. "We've been over this and we have very different takes on my favorite movie. But I forgive you."

Jenna lives in a big house in the country. It's a calculated risk driving that way. Still, the party noises on the other end of the phone line sure sounded inviting.

No sooner am I on the dark highway toward Jenna's than I know this was a bad idea. My car is fishtailing on the snow and ice. Damn these old tires. I recover from the skid and go slower.

But the wind is picking up even more. The snow is peppering the windshield so fast, all I can see is white.

My eyes are barely able to identify black patches of pavement to guide me; it's going to be five miles per hour from here until safety. I turn on my hazards and white knuckle the steering wheel.

Out of nowhere, my car comes to a complete stop. My foot is still on the gas, but the wheels are not moving. That's when I notice my front end is completely covered in a snow drift.

I hadn't even realized I'd left the road and gone into the ditch. That's how disorienting the white-out driving can be. I should know better; I just warned my viewers at home about this exact scenario.

Well, isn't this a nice bit of luck.

I try to think what to do next. I can't call for help. The police and deputies likely are all over the county helping people in true danger.

I'm not worried, though. I can survive for days in my car with my survival kit: blanket, pillow, a box of Snickers bars, a box of Cheez-its, water, a flashlight, batteries, a flare and most importantly, various other necessities, and a bottle of vodka.

If my weather predictions are correct today, the blizzard should be past us by morning. As long as no other motorist hits me with their vehicle, I should be fine to camp out here in my car for the night.

I entertain myself by reading a book on my e-reader for about an hour. I begin to shiver and I turn on the engine to warm up a bit, but only for a few minutes. I need to save fuel and save the car battery.

I decide to do a live social media video to pass the time.

It's not the best idea to suck up my phone battery, but I do have a juiced up phone charger that doesn't need to be plugged in. I do a quick, one-minute video, explaining to all the people on my page that I am stuck in a snow drift, but not to worry because I'm perfectly prepared. The likes, hearts, sad and shocked faces are exploding all over my phone screen. It's very sweet and I'd love nothing more to interact with my people, but ultimately it's best if I turn off data for now. I never know what might happen, so I need every second of battery life in case of emergency.

One thing I have not prepared for was having to go to the bathroom. I mean, I have toilet paper, and I have means to sanitize my hands. But I guess I never thought about how exactly a girl goes to the bathroom in a severe snowstorm.

Maybe I can hold it until morning.

Nope. Definitely cannot do that.

I bite my lip and look around at the direction the wind is coming from. I cannot even see the road now. By the way the car is angled, I'm guessing that the passenger side is more or less facing the ditch, which is, of course, filled with several feet of snow and probably the reason my car did not get banged up in the process of getting stuck. That side of the car appears to be the least exposed to the wind, so I act. I grab my supplies and scoot over to the passenger side and open the door.

While I'm outside the car, getting battered by the wind and flying snow, I am at least thankful that Jenna let everyone dress casual today and I don't have to navigate this horrible night in a skirt suit. Second, I'm grateful that Jenna is my size and will likely have clothes I can borrow as soon as I arrive.

I finish up what I'm doing as quickly as I can.

Just as abruptly as my car hitting the snow bank in the ditch, a pair of headlights blind me.

One second I'm completely lost in a winter wilderness in the blackest night, and the next second, some big-ass truck is bearing down on me.

Not a semi truck. Not a city snow plow, either.

It looks like a monster truck. The tires are like those of a tractor. This is an impossibly jacked up thing. No, wait. It's a tow truck. Hallelujah! I might get to Jenna's party yet.

CHAPTER 3

Bear

So far tonight, I've picked up a car load of college kids trying to bar crawl their way through the blizzard. They'd gotten their car stuck in a snowdrift at the city pedestrian plaza. Fortunately, their car started just fine and wasn't stuck too badly. I pulled them out and warned them to get themselves home. Slowly. And with a sober driver.

I stopped by a few accidents where I saw the police already handling the situation. Only one needed my assistance. All the ambulances were busy, so I drove one accident victim to the emergency room to get checked out.

For the most part, people seem to be staying off the roads, which is a good thing.

"Guess I'm not the only one who listens to Mary Reed," I say to myself.

Before the words are out of my mouth I see an alert on my phone.

Mary Reed has posted a live video. Yes, I do have push

notifications in place for any and all of her updates. Are you surprised?

I slow to a complete stop while I watch the video. It's a shot of her face and she's in her car, looking as perky and beautiful as ever. "I have a confession to make. I don't want anyone to worry but I'm stuck in a snow bank on Highway 61 outside of town. That's right folks, I didn't take my own advice. But I don't want you to worry, I have food and water and I'm completely fine."

My blood runs cold.

She might be a plucky little female who knows how to handle herself, but something comes over me. I cannot let her stay out in this mess. Alone.

I toss my phone aside and get going. I'm on my way to find my weather girl.

I make my way to Highway 61 while wondering what the hell she's doing all the way out there when everybody knows she lives downtown near the television station. Not that I've ever driven past her house for no reason. OK maybe like twice a week.

Soon enough I'm on the highway,

And there it is. A green car off in the distance. Not that I know what Mary Reed's car looks like. Only a weirdo would make an effort to know what his TV crush's car looks like.

Although these are white-out conditions, from up here in the cab, I can see OK. There's a person, a female, standing outside. pulling up her jeans. The car's hazard lights are blinking.

Female, alone at night, on the road, outside of town? This is not good. Suspecting that this female is Mary Reed triggers my protective side to a whole other level.

I start to slow way down as I get closer.

Sweet Lord, it *is* Mary Reed. I know I was specifically

looking for her but I can't believe it was so easy to find her. I don't believe in destiny, but this feels like it.

I ease the truck to a stop behind her car, and then I see her face. She's got a heavy coat, boots, hat and hood on, but she's got my heart pounding outside of my chest. I'd know those eyes and that smile from a mile away. In real life, even in a snowstorm, my weather girl is not just beautiful. She's phenomenal.

You know what else I can spot from a mile away?

A Christmas present from the Universe.

CHAPTER 4

Mary

Curiously, the tow truck driver is exiting via the passenger side door.

In one swift cat-like move he's out of his truck and running past me and opening the driver door of my car.

For half a second I wonder if I'm about to be carjacked.

But I realize how preposterous that is in the middle of a snowstorm. I see the writing "Bear Bailey Towing" on the side of the truck. Bailey? Seriously?

Well, there's no way anybody with a tow truck business would want to steal my car. I see that he's turning off my hazards, grabbing my blanket and emergency kit.

The next half second I'm preoccupied with the thought that he might be stealing from me. But again, that doesn't seem likely.

Just when I wonder what's going to happen next, he's got me in his arms. He literally scoops me up off my feet, and he's lifting me up into the cab of his truck like I weigh nothing.

It's hard to determine his features while my eyes are being pelted with snow, but his arms are strong and he's tall and lean, even under the work overalls and coat he's wearing. Nobody has ever swept me off my feet before and I can't lie, it gives me a tiny thrill. I'm a modern woman and all, but a little bit of chivalry on Christmas Eve lights a warm little cinder in my belly.

The driver gently but quickly sets me into the cab and then follows me inside, slamming the door.

"You don't need to…" I start, but I can't finish because I'm speechless. This man is climbing on top of me.

I gasp.

He gruffly says, "Driver side door is frozen shut. Just trying to switch places with you, unless you know how to drive stick, Mary Reed."

My mouth forms an O, but I don't make any noise because I don't know whether to be embarrassed by my own assumptions or by the fact that his abdomen sweeping hard across mine has awakened a latent arousal in me.

I wiggle this way, he inches that way, and soon we've successfully switched seats.

"Thought it would be easier this way than me turning into a popsicle while trying to get it open," he says. "Sorry if that was a little too close for comfort."

It occurs to me that he could have entered the truck first and pulled me in, but I'm still feeling tingly all over from being in his arms. Even if he is a total stranger.

Because, he's a nice stranger. A tall, strong stranger.

He's buckling me in. I protest, but he's just doing it anyway. "I can buckle…you don't have to do that…"

Click.

His hand is still on the seat belt clip by my hip and his other hand is adjusting the strap at my opposite shoulder.

It's now that I get a good look at his face.

Whoa.

And then he grins at me and says, "Bear. Bear Bailey. Nice to meet you. You OK?" His full lips when they smile are full of mischief but not threatening, and he's got the kind of creases all over his forehead and by his eyes that betray the kindest of natures. Just like my Jimmy Stewart.

Don't do that, Mary, I say to myself. Don't go equating helpful tow truck drivers with your fantasy dreamboat.

"Your last name is Bailey?"

He nods. "As in all things Christmas. Irish cream and George."

I blush.

A news chyron flashes through my head before I can stop it. "Bear Bailey: hottest of all the tow truck drivers in the city? Take our Twitter poll! #stonefoxtowtruckdriver."

He has flashing irises that remind me of a warm fireplace. He has full, sharp eyebrows that are knitted together in concern. A nice nose that looks like it's seen a few fists or close contact with a football tackle in its time. His jawline and cheekbones look like you could cut paper on them.

I catch myself getting lost in his eyes for a minute, and dammit if the walls of my sex don't contract in response.

He sees my cheeks flush in reaction to him and his grin goes bigger. His teeth are nice, but he has a charmingly crooked front tooth. His lips are oh-so nice to look at, full and luscious enough to be the envy of any pouty-lipped male model. He has shy little dimple, just on one cheek. I can't decide if the look he's giving me is full bad boy or charming do-gooder.

Sweet Lord. Bear Bailey is half old-timey World War II hero and half ruffian. And 100 percent under my skin.

CHAPTER 5

Bear

"I'm Mary. Mary Reed. You must have seen my video and found me. But you know, I didn't call for a tow," she says.

I smile at her and finally let go of her seat belt. Her cheeks are flushed and her hair is damp where it's peeking out from under her stocking cap.

I ignore her remark about not calling for a tow. "I'm glad to see you own a winter hat," I say. "I worry about you, the way you stand outside in the freezing cold in front of the camera."

She's been outside long enough to get pummeled by the wind and snow, and I wish I had something to take the chill off.

Well, I do, in fact, have a very large something to take the chill off, but she's not ready for that yet.

I know, what a creepy thing to think in the 30 seconds after helping someone. But damn. Being this close to her and feeling what I'm feeling...and it's been a long time since...well let's just say it's hard not to think about getting her into my warm bed.

I rifle through her emergency kit to find something other than my body to warm her up. She's got junk food, water and vodka. "Well, you prepared for a party," I say.

She seems agitated the more I riffle around in the kit. "Um yes, there's nothing else in there…"

I grab on to the end of something that looks like a flashlight. It's purple and has a button on the end of the handle. "Flashlight?"

"Um, it's…" she says. "My massager. Never mind that, it's just a neck massager that helps with migraines."

When I click the button, no light comes on, but it vibrates. And that's when I see the silhouette of it in the darkness.

"Oh," I say, "how do I turn this off…"

She grabs for it in the dark. "Here, you just click it two more times and… OK, it's off. Oh my god."

I toss my head back and laugh. Her face turns three shades of crimson. "Wow, you really aren't messing around with your emergency kit."

"Nope. I mean yep. I mean, shut up, let's go."

I shrug and throw the truck into gear. "No big deal. Nice to know my favorite local weather girl is actually a human being."

Her cheeks are so red they're almost pulsating.

But it doesn't change the fact that Mary Reed is ten times as beautiful in person as she is on TV.

"I'm extremely human. I'm so human I can't pay you for a tow. Christmas presents pretty much broke the bank this year," she says.

"Well, then it's a good thing I can't tow your car out until morning. Not safe for me to be towing vehicles on these country roads."

This is sort of a lie. I could effortlessly hook up her little Toyota and safely drop it at the garage tonight as well as see her home safely. But I don't want her driving anywhere else tonight. Something tells me she might be the kind of woman with a one-track mind.

Too bad, because I'm not letting her out of my sight.

"OK, so you're…what? Giving me a ride out of the goodness of your heart?"

I nod. "Exactly. Where were you headed? And why? I do believe I saw your weather report earlier tonight, warning everyone to not do exactly what you were just doing."

She sighs. "I was just going to go home and be alone tonight as usual, but then…then I changed my mind and wanted to go see my friend Jenna. She lives on Black Angus Trail. Thought I'd ride out the blizzard with her and some friends."

"What kind of friends would have you drive in a blizzard?"

"Drunk friends. Fun friends. Friends trying to set me up on dates," she says.

I've never had this kind of reaction to the idea of an attractive girl being hit on by someone else before, but suddenly I've got the primal urge to take charge of tonight.

"Oh, that is absolutely not happening tonight, my weather girl," I say.

She shifts in her seat.

"First of all, you can stop calling me 'weather girl.' I graduated with honors, I'll have you know. You can just call me Mary. Second, yes, you can take me to that party. In fact, I'll put it into your GPS right now." Her hand searches the dash futilely.

I bite out, "Ain't got GPS in here. The Snow Angel knows its way by memory anywhere you want to go in this county. And it doesn't matter. There is no way I'm taking my weather girl to a blizzard party with a bunch of drunk, single people. No way."

I navigate my way back toward town and hope she doesn't object too strongly.

Doesn't matter if she does or not. She clearly doesn't know how to keep herself safe.

And that's fine. I'll be seeing to that from now on.

CHAPTER 6

Mary

I'm not entirely sure where he's taking me, but then again, I'm not sure if we're driving on an actual road. Or if this truck is still right side up or in the Upside Down World from *Stranger Things*.

My body heat is doing its thing now. Combined with the heat blasting from the vents in Bear Bailey's truck cab. I take off my hood and my hat, unbuttoning and wiggling out of my overcoat. I comb out my snow- and sweat-damp hair with my fingers. I am a hot mess of melted snow and fruity-smelling hairspray.

While I do this, I think I hear a low, quiet growl coming from the driver seat.

I glance over and see that Bear has his eyes on the road. He looks normal, other than the fact that he's yanking off his stocking cap and unzipping his coat.

His hair is also damp and his face is flushed.

"So what are you doing out here in this weather, just rescuing people out of the insane goodness of your heart?" I ask.

He says, "Got nothing else to do on a Christmas Eve. People are trying to get where they're going. They might need help. I have the truck to help them."

I bite my lip as I try not to let this warm my heart too much. It does anyway. "I bet your wife or girlfriend would disagree with that."

I see Bear smirk. "No wife. No girlfriend. Nice interview technique you got there, though. You could have just asked if I was single, like I was about to ask you."

Something invisible flutters with delight down deep between my legs. Bear's interest in me is becoming clearer. All the logical parts of me tell me he could be a creep. But somehow, I know he's not.

"I find it hard to believe you're single," I say, regretting it as soon as it's out of my mouth. I instantly feel ashamed about being too forward.

But Bear doesn't react other than to glance over at me and show that little dimple again. His sandy, stubbly chin looks as sweet as a Christmas cookie. One I'd really like to take a nibble out of.

We are flirting now, aren't we? This is outright, blatant flirting. I haven't done this in earnest in…well I don't know if I've ever blatantly flirted with a man. Boys? Yes. Men? Never.

I'm 26 and in the middle of an upward career climb, which doesn't give me much time to date.

Bear, however, is clearly good at this.

"Oh, I see. You're a player, is that it? I should have guessed," I say.

I'm only half joking. But his face turns dark.

"Not at all," he says.

"Are you kidding? Look at you! You must have girls lined up around the block waiting to go out with you."

He slows the truck to a crawl and looks me straight in the face. "You like the way I look?"

I bite my lip. "It's not entirely unpleasant."

He laughs. "Glad to know that."

I persist. "So tell me how it's possible you're not attached. Some chick do you wrong?"

The smile disappears from his lips and his face goes darker than before. Oh, yeah. There's a story there.

He's just not ready to tell it yet.

He reaches over and I think he's going to grab my leg. My breath catches.

"Relax," he says, opening the glove box. "Grab that CD and pop it in. This will explain why I'm still single."

I do as he says, and something totally unexpected happens. After a few moments, I hear the soundtrack to the Walt Disney adaptation of Charles Dickens' *A Christmas Carol.*

"Oh my gosh," I gasp. "I used to have this record when I was a kid, and I wore it out!"

He smiles. "My favorite thing to listen to at Christmastime."

I squeal like a little girl, but I'm too excited to be embarrassed as childhood memories come flooding back. "Whenever I heard Goofy's Jacob Marley, and those spooky chains coming up the stairs, I had to jump onto my bed and pull the covers over me. I was afraid something was going to grab my ankles. Is that weird?"

Bear's smile is getting so big he's beaming.

"Not as weird as this," he says, and then all of a sudden he launches into all the voices in sync with the CD, doing both Scrooge McDuck with a perfect Scottish accent and the full squawking Donald Duck voice as nephew Fred.

"Merry Christmas!" he quacks.

Oh. My. God.

This is a little weird, but…

I don't think I've ever wanted a man more.

CHAPTER 7

Bear

*Y*eah, it's a little weird but…

I have to put on the Disney CD to defuse the sexual tension.

The way she just peeled off her coat and hat. Shit on a fruitcake. Her little body hiding underneath that coat is even cuter than on television. Because, of course it is.

Her breasts in that red sweater are now live and three-dimensional now. Her face is relaxed and doesn't have that authoritative air that she has live on the air. Though, I gotta admit, I kinda like that authoritative air about her.

I catch her eye while she's laughing at my line-by-line mimicry, and her eyes are wide in surprise, but also fascinated. As I keep going with the Scrooge McDuck "Bah! Humbug!" speech, she's soon doubled over and putting a hand to her chest.

I thought all of this would make my impure thoughts about her calm down. Dirty thoughts. Filthy thoughts.

But the sound of her laughter and knowing I made it happen, it's making everything worse.

She's got an incredibly sexy laugh, like small shards of pure ice tumbling into a whiskey glass.

It makes me wonder what her voice will sound like when I take her in my bed.

She keeps laughing like that, we're not gonna be able to wait until we get to my bed. It's gonna happen right here in the cab of my truck.

I can't stop making her laugh, though. Pretty soon, she's dabbing at her eyes.

"I thought I was fine waiting out the storm alone in my car, but this is a Christmas miracle," she says, sitting up and catching her breath. "I love you!"

I stop my silly antics and put my eyes back on the road. She covers her mouth in shock at herself. "I mean I love your sense of humor. I love people…with your sense of humor."

The smirk that crosses my face is untamable. I say, "I know exactly what you meant."

I'm not totally sure how to transition from here.

Which is probably why the Universe just sent me my next Christmas wish. Another stranded traveler on the road.

CHAPTER 8

Mary

I open my door and I'm about to hop out of his way, assuming the driver side door is still getting pelted by the wind, snow and ice. But then Bear grabs both my arms.

I gasp as I'm suddenly in the air. He is once again lifting me, this time over his lap as he scoots himself out underneath me. He plops me down on the driver side, and I think I hear him mutter, "No way I'm letting my weather girl get snow and ice on her again."

My heart skips a beat at this bossy side of him. He's done enough—pulled me out of the snowstorm, kept me warm, made me laugh, flirted with me in a way that isn't even creepy at all—but his increasing protectiveness of me is feeling more and more erotic as the night wears on.

I see him grab a large ice scraper with a metal edge before he hops out.

"Let me know if I can be of any—"

But before I can finish that sentence, he casts up a warning look. His wolfish eyes are telling me to stay put. Normally, I am not compelled to listen to anybody who's so bossy with me. But with him, it works.

It's ridiculous that I'm listening to him. I'm a helpful person, almost to a fault.

So, am I just going to let him keep me shut up in this cab?

Yes. Yes, I am.

I watch him move around through the blinding snow. There seems to be only one passenger, and she's done a 180 in her Lincoln Continental right on the ice and can't seem to get enough traction to get the tires moving in the right direction. When the wind lets up for half a second to reveal the night sky, the headlights shine on a road sign. My brain tracks to our location. We're headed back into town. I finally accept that I'm not going to make it to any party, but I should at least let Jenna know what's going on.

I take out my phone and text her: *Car stuck in snow. No damage. Did you see my vid? Rando tow truck driver picked me up. Funny story—he's out here on the roads all night long helping stranded drivers, for FREE. What?! I know. He's...pretty hot, IMO. Weird night.*

Jenna texts back shortly: *OMG. I hope that's not just a line to make you think he's a nice guy. But I trust your instincts.*

I text her back to say I'll let her know as soon as we end up where we're going…wherever that might be.

The person that piles into the back seat of the crew cab is not actually an old woman. I had only assumed this because I saw a blonde wig and the Lincoln. Now that I see this person up close, it's actually a very famous local drag artist, Violet Bick. She's wearing a luxe purple overcoat and boots with heels as high as heaven. She buckles herself in and shouts, "It's colder than a witch's titty out there!"

I turn in my seat and gape at her. "Ms. Bick, Merry Christmas!"

She returns my smile and extends a hand covered in a fur-lined leather glove. She apologizes for nothing; that leather and that fur is real. I squeeze her hand.

"You can just call me Violet," she says.

"We've met before," I say. "I did a live feed at your club after the tornadoes came through last year. You were doing a supply drive for people who had lost their homes."

Bear has hooked up the Lincoln to the tow line and has chipped away at the ice holding the driver side door closed. He's cussing as he piles in, slamming the door against the rushing wind. He cranks the heat and pulls off his ice-covered gloves, blows on them.

Violet's glittered eyelids pop as recognition floods her face. "Oh my god, Chief Meteorologist Mary Reed from Channel 2!"

I laugh as I give Bear an elbow. "Did you hear that? She knows my proper title!"

Bear turns and nods to Violet politely and looks at me. "That's all right by me. I'm the only one allowed to call you my weather girl."

I cluck my tongue at him. "It's a little sexist, don't you think?"

Violet is checking the state of her wig in a compact mirror and picking out tiny chunks of snow. "Oh, you two are too young to be arguing like old marrieds. How long y'all been together?"

My heart drops into my stomach and then lurches up into my throat. It's like being on a rollercoaster. I look over at Bear and I laugh. "We're not together," I say.

Bear mutters for only me to hear, "Not yet anyway." His rough voice does things to me. Specifically, my nipples. They could chip away at ice all on their own when he mutters things about me under his breath. God, it's been too long. Obviously my body does not care that my brain is tossing up warning flares left and right.

"Well," Violet says, waving off the awkwardness in the air. "You two are just too adorable not to be hitting that. Girl, you are gonna hit that, right?"

I cover my mouth and feel heat crawling up my chest and neck. "I, uh…"

Violet checks over her teeth for lipstick and does not seem at all fazed by my reaction. I glance at Bear and he doesn't either.

I search for words, but Bear fills in the space for me as he wheels the tow truck back on the road into town. "Where you headed, Violet?"

Violet claps her compact closed and drops it into a sequined bag that I might be drooling over as much as I'm drooling over the tow truck driver. "Well, I just finished one show at the Soda Jerk," she says, referring to the city's most popular drag bar that used to be a candy store and apothecary back in the day, which she now owns. "And I'm supposed to be caroling at the nursing home with the rest of my sisters tonight."

My mouth falls open. "That's amazing! I'll be brutally honest, I'm impressed that those people of that generation would…you know…be welcoming to…"

Violet cocks her head. "To a bunch of boys in drag singing about Christmas? Honey, you'd be surprised how people's opinions change when they don't get many visitors."

I turn to look at Bear. His eyes are fiercely glued to the road. His Adam's apple just rolled like he's swallowing something back and he's chewing on his lip. I feel it too and I have to bite the inside of my cheek. I can't have Violet see me cry.

Violet announces that she's going to make some calls to

her fellow carolers. I tune out the sound of her voice with the guilty feelings in my head.

This is all wrong. How can I be thinking about sex on a night like tonight? When there are homeless people, people in hospitals and nursing homes, who have real needs tonight?

"My house is not far from the nursing home. If you want to drop me off," I say, meekly, staring into my hands that rest on my lap.

Bear looks over at me, and the hunger in his blazing warm eyes feel like he's already got me on my back in his bed.

"Nope," he says.

"Oh," I breathe.

I should not have any doubt what his intentions are at this point.

But my mouth. My stupid mouth. It cannot stop talking. "Well, where do you want to take—"

I generally do not enjoy being interrupted.

Bear Bailey has the nicest way of interrupting.

He closes in fast. His lips are a hair's breadth away from mine. He's so close I can feel his breath on me. I can feel the electricity sparking from his skin to mine. His nose has got to be smelling my skin at this proximity.

I can smell him too. Chapstick, some kind of masculine, woodsy lotion. Strong, black coffee.

I want to keep talking because I'm nervous, but if I move my lips, they'll be touching his. And I don't want to be the one to initiate any kissing. No reason other than on principle.

And then he speaks. "I ain't taking you home tonight, in case you haven't figured it out yet."

My breath is shaky. "I had a feeling."

Somehow our lips are touching, but we're not kissing yet.

His eyes are on mine, and then on my cheeks, my hair, my neck, my chin. Like he can't decide where to kiss me first.

"I like you," he says against my forehead. His breath ripples against the baby fine hairs along my hairline.

"I know," I say.

"Usually, I go slow and do something like this first," he says, picking up my hand that's resting on my leg. Facing me, he laces the fingers of his left hand through my fingers. He pulls my hand up and kisses every one of my knuckles. My lips part at the sensation. His lips are so soft, and so are his whiskers against my skin.

When he reaches my fifth knuckle, I'm pretty sure he's gonna kiss me.

But then, his phone rings.

He grits out, "Dammit."

He grabs it off the dash and answers it. "Yeah."

The voice on the other end sounds official. All I hear is something about a mother and a minivan. His brows knit together in concern. He looks up at me. All thought of kissing me is right out the window, something big is going on.

CHAPTER 9

Mary

"I think I see the minivan up ahead," Bear says. "They don't look stuck though, maybe just broke down."

"That's not good. She could be freezing in there if the engine isn't working," I agree.

"I was thinking the same thing," he replies.

"You two do realize you are now on a mission together. This thing between you two is, like, happening. Mmkay?" Violet is finally off the phone with her friends and back to telling us what's what.

I look over, and Bear is trying to concentrate on pulling over safely but also smirking.

"Would be a great story to tell our grandkids."

Violet hoots from the back seat.

I can't even respond. Anybody else saying that to me would send me packing.

His words and that sweet sideways smile as he cocks his head after he says something daring… I just melt.

It's a little nuts. It's way too fast.

But I just…feel it.

We pull ahead and come to a stop in front of the minivan.

As we pass, I see that the interior lights of the vehicle are on. There is a man and a woman in the back seat. I can't make out what is going on, but something inside me is telling me the woman is in trouble.

"Stay put," Bear says again. Though this time, he squeezes my knee and his voice is reassuring. My skin crackles where he touches my jeans.

I watch him hop out like a damn superhero and I have to remind myself this is a rescue mission on Christmas Eve, not a sexy summer road trip. No matter how much heat I can feel between my legs.

"Don't think too hard about it, honey."

I turn in my seat to face Violet.

"That's all I do is think."

"You all just make sense. You all are good people and you need to get together and start making more nice, good, helpful people."

Damn if I don't get a tear in the corner of my eye. Violet had a way of cutting through the bullshit. The conventions of how long Bear and I have known each other doesn't seem to matter anymore.

"He is a good man," I say, my voice cracking.

My head swings around as my door pops open. Bear looks worried. "Coats, blankets, and all hands on deck."

Violet and I don't ask any questions. We haul ass out of the truck with all of our bags and emergency kits, with Bear's help.

We all pile into the minivan and see that the woman is indeed having a problem.

"She's having a baby right now!" I say.

"Mr. Bear, we gotta get this lady to the hospital," Violet says.

"There's no time," says the woman, panting. She locks eyes with me. "Help me get ready?"

I nod at her. "You and the baby are gonna be fine."

Even though I've never done this before.

Even though I'm scared out of my mind.

Something takes over. I'd like to imagine it's my midwife great-great grandmother's DNA taking over. Or just a natural instinct.

Or just the need to keep her calm.

I tell the man with her to lower the back of the bench seat into a bed, which he does.

I help her remove her leggings and get as comfortable as possible.

The man with her is holding her hand on one side. Violet has stationed herself at the woman's other side and is holding her other hand.

Bear is pulling all of the things out of my and Violet's bags and emergency kits that might be of use.

He hands me several blankets, scarves and sweaters.

"I don't know about breathing through a contraction, but I do know yoga breathing," I say.

The woman nods and shouts, "Here one comes!"

I tell her, "Eyes on me, mama. Breathe in as slowly as you can, as deeply as you can."

She sobs and screams.

"Come on, mama, you can do it."

I don't think personally that I could do this if I were delivering my own baby in the back of a minivan during a snowstorm, but this is the kind of thing you say, right?

She nods and sucks in a breath slowly.

"Good, now just take two more sips of air. One. Two.

Good. Now pretend you're a leaky tire and blow it out slowly out of your mouth."

I can tell the contraction has subsided because her face relaxes.

Suddenly her eyes pop wide at me. "Oh my god, you're Chief Meteorologist Mary Reed! Jacob, Mary Reed is delivering our baby in a snowstorm!"

But Jacob has no time to react because the woman's hand is clamping down like a vise on his hand. Her face scrunches up in pain because another contraction is here.

"Nice to meet you. And you are?"

"Gah! Liz!"

"Breathe in through your nose, Liz," I say.

A hand presses on my back. I look to my left and it's Bear. "Sweetheart," he says. His eyes are not on me but on the business between Liz's legs.

I follow his gaze and I see what he's seeing. It's the baby's head.

I put my hand on his and say, "Hand sanitizer. In my bag."

He's got it to me in half a second and I do my best to get clean. "Liz, sweetie? Time to push."

Liz gives only three massive pushes and the baby is out and in my arms.

"Oh my god, you have a baby girl!"

I wrap the baby up as best I can and make sure her tiny air pathways are clear. She squeaks, and it's just a precursor leading up to a huge squall. As quickly as possible I hand the baby off to Liz and Jacob. Bear hands a water bottle over to Violet and I do my best to ruin more of my things than any of Violet's fabulous things as I'm dealing with the aftermath.

I look up and Violet is sobbing, Liz is sobbing with happiness and Bear is shaking Jacob's hand.

"Congrats, man."

CHAPTER 10

Bear

Mercifully, the wind lets up briefly so we can move Liz, the baby and Jacob into the back seat of my truck. Violet joins us in the front seat and that means my weather girl has to squeeze in extra close to me.

This being a manual transmission, the closeness gets real interesting.

I have to reach between Mary's knees to shift gears.

"I can't believe what just happened," she says, looking so dazed that my hand between her knees doesn't seem to register.

"I can," I say. "You delivered a baby. You're amazing."

As I concentrate on the road I see her shaking her head. "I barely did anything."

Violet scoffs. "You were large and in charge, I'm not buying this false modesty."

I hear her sniffle. "Liz did all the work."

I think maybe she's getting emotional and I want so bad to put my arms around her. Damn this gear shift.

Day after Christmas I'm selling this hunk of junk and getting an automatic.

"You were great. You all were great," Liz says.

I can hear the baby nursing at her mother's breast and it makes my heart clench in my chest.

This is what I want. Not to have a baby by the side of the road in a snowstorm, of course. A family. With Mary Reed. My weather girl.

"I'm gonna get us to the hospital, Liz," I say.

"Thank you," says Jacob.

That's it. I can't take it anymore. My heart is so full, I just can't not kiss this woman. I let go of the gear shift and cup her face. I pull her close. I murmur in her ear, "I have a secret."

She breathes and waits.

"You're coming home with me," I say.

I feel her cheek heat up between my fingers. "Yes, I think we already figure out that I'm coming home with you tonight," she whispers.

"That's not exactly what I meant. I mean every night."

"Oh," she whispers. "Oh my god, look out!"

I tap the brakes and just miss it.

The four-legged creature is in the middle of the road.

It's covered in snow and it's not moving.

"Shit, what is that?" Violet says.

"Somebody lose a camel?" I grunt huskily, cursing every interruption so far this evening.

"It's so small, it has gotta be missing its mother," Mary says. "What's it doing in the middle of town? We have to help it."

"I love you for wanting to help, but baby, we got a brand

new infant in this truck. Animals wreak havoc. Germs and shit."

Liz speaks up from the back seat. "You get that baby camel in this truck right now or I'm walking baby Mary-Violet the rest of the way to the hospital."

My weather girl grips her heart. "You named her Mary-Violet?" Her voice is cracking. "That is so sweet!"

"I may be sweet, but listen, I was raised on a farm and I spent most of my childhood in a barn with baby goats. We are not scared of baby camel germs," Liz says.

I look over at Mary. She's pouting.

How can I say no to a brand new mother who's just given birth, or to my weather girl?

"Guess you're outnumbered," Mary says with a shrug.

"Shit," I mutter. "I was outnumbered the second I put you in my truck."

She starts to pull on her coat. "It might get a little rough out there, so I'm gonna help you. Violet, you mind getting in the back so we can at least keep the camel away from the baby?"

CHAPTER 11

Mary

Almost as soon as we approach the trembling little camel calf, we notice she's wearing a tiny bridle, and her reins are hanging loose.

The calf is frightened; too frightened to come with us on her own motivation. She's lost and confused.

And then, out of the blinding snow, comes another figure. It looks like a man. Dressed in…a bathrobe?

The strange man approaches, and I have to yell to be heard over the noise of the pounding wind.

"My camel," is all he says.

"Get in the truck!" Bear shouts over the din.

Moments later, the man in the robes is sitting next to me, with a baby camel on his lap.

Violet is in back, tucked in next to the baby and the family.

And where does that leave me?

Nowhere left to sit but on Bear's lap.

Yep.

When we're all settled in, into the weirdest assembly of passengers known to man on Christmas Eve night, I have to ask. I'm dying to know what's going on here.

"So, spill it. What are you doing out here in a bathrobe with a baby camel?" I ask.

"We had to pack up the live nativity early. My wife stayed with the animal trailer. Essie, the baby here, bolted when the snow started falling. I've been looking for her for hours."

"In a bathrobe?" I say.

"Well, I've got boots and snow pants under the robes. Look, the whole ensemble makes more sense when I've got my crown," he says, putting out a hand. "Trey. Trey Wiseman."

The man called Trey takes out his phone. "I'd better let the my wife know what happened to me."

I fiddle with the heater to blow warm air directly onto Wiseman and his little camel.

She mewls meekly.

This night is getting weirder by the second.

The plow is scraping away at the snow and ice on the road in front of us.

We are inching along the road, and my phone's GPS, which Bear has finally agreed to let me use, tells us we are about a mile from the hospital now.

Trey is petting his camel and speaking to her softly. Violet seems to be snoring in the back seat. The family with the baby is obviously enthralled with their little miracle.

And Bear has got one arm around my waist with his hand on the gear shift.

His other hand is on the steering wheel and I'm sitting across his lap with one arm around his shoulders.

My left breast is dangerously close to his sandy whiskers. I find my thoughts wandering, wishing I could feel those whiskers against my bare skin. My nipples turn into little pebbles beneath my sweater.

Bear's strong jaw is rippling, like he's angry. Or frustrated with something.

Under my legs, I can feel the large rod, all the way through his rough canvas snow pants.

If I'm not mistaken, I can hear a faint, guttural growl coming from the back of Bear's throat.

I study his face and he looks like keeping his eyes on the road is literally causing him pain.

"You OK?" I ask in a low whisper.

He nods and says, "C'mere, I need to say something."

I bend my ear close to his lips. His breath is warm and he's so close I can feel his bristles brush the back of my jawbone and my throat.

"I got a powerful ache because of you. Before this night is over I'm gonna take you so damn hard."

I bite my lip and try not to moan as I feel my sex contract in pleasure. His voice sends shivers down my neck, my sternum and has turned my nipples into taut little buds.

I dare to kiss him right at the back of his jaw, below his ear, and I murmur, just loud enough for him to hear, "Let me steer. You can do what you want with that hand. Nobody can see anything from this angle."

He grunts, but quietly.

Bear lets go of the wheel and I put my hand on it, my eyes on the road, as much of it as I can make out, anyway.

Bear's free hand glides up my thigh. My long, puffy coat is still on from the last time I hopped out of the truck, so nobody can see when his fingers reach the hottest area between my thighs.

The camel is mewling, people are talking and Violet is snoring, so nobody can hear Bear whisper raggedly as I steer.

"Damn. You're already wet for me under those jeans, aren't you, weather girl?"

"Umm," I say softly. I unzip my puffy coat all the way down to give Bear better access. "There's only one way to find out, but so sorry, I can't unzip my jeans right now."

He whispers back. "It's all right. I've got one nipple in my face and one hand between your legs. That's all I need to give my girl what she wants.'

I laugh and reply, "That would be a cute trick. But there's no way."

Bear raises one eyebrow and shoots me a look that makes my cheeks heat up. His fingers accept the challenge.

Bear

I have to control myself unless I want every passenger, human and animal, in the car to hear me growl like an animal.

I can most definitely give my weather girl an orgasm by doing what I'm doing right now—stroking her pussy through her jeans with one hand and raking her nipple through her sweater with my teeth.

It sure as hell isn't going to ease the ache in my pants, but it's hot as hell.

Little Bear is getting more urgent and angrier with me the more I play with the sultry female who's across my lap as if she's a rag doll serving at my pleasure.

I just can't stop touching her.

And bless her and damn her for taking the wheel.

This is both insanely hot and sensual but also really goddamn frustrating.

It's not fair, the more I scrape her and nip at the soft

fabric that covers her tit, the harder my cock gets. She's my little Christmas cookie, and the icing is in danger of ending up all over the inside of my pants.

Instead of where it belongs. On my weather girl.

Make that *inside* my weather girl.

My fingers work her over, and although I can't feel her clit, I feel her very slightly rock her pelvis into me. She's guiding her sweet spot into my rough, hard-working fingers.

At the same time, my head is dipping down, my mouth completely soaking the fabric of her sweater where her left breast is. I can nearly smell her ripe skin.

The sweater is taunting me. I ache to feel the skin underneath all these layers.

The surging desire to lay her down, spread her wide and have my way with her entirely naked body is overwhelming.

To feel her pussy. Is it shaved bare or not? Doesn't bother me either way, as long as it's mine.

To taste her there.

If it's anything like the subtle scent of spices and figs on her skin, I'm going to enjoy ravishing her with my mouth.

And once I take her like that, I know I'm going to never let her leave.

She's going to stay put and I'm going to devour her like that every night. Maybe every morning too. Maybe every afternoon.

Any minute of the day we're together, is what I'm trying to say.

I whisper so nobody else can hear. "Have you ever tasted yourself? I bet it's good."

She's biting her lip again. Shit, if she only knew what that does to me.

She doesn't say anything but keeps her eyes on the road and shakes her head.

"Want me to stop talking like this?"

She shakes her head ever so slightly again,

My hand on her pussy moves more urgently, massaging her harder and in wide, pleasurable circles. I see her slightly flutter her eyes closed, though she's doing her best to keep her eyes on the road.

"You're wetting yourself through your jeans, weather girl. It's got my fingers even a little wet. Let's have a taste."

Her breath catches as I bring my fingers to my mouth and suck the ends.

"I was right," I say. "My weather girl wants me bad."

With that, I squeeze her mound assertively and take her protruding nipple into my mouth.

My girl loses control and grips the wheel with whitened knuckles. The fingers of her other hand are digging into my shoulder. She's biting down hard on her lips so as not to make a sound, so hard her lips are turning white. Her eyes are closed and her hips have slammed into my hand. Her whole body shudders. She's trying so hard to make no noise as the climax washes over her.

"Easy, baby. I got you. Let it out."

She rides out the rest of her orgasm by pretending to sneeze and then laugh about it.

"Hoo, that was a big one!" she says aloud, for everyone else's benefit.

There's a chorus of "bless you"s, and when she's satisfied nobody could tell what we just did, she relaxes back against my chest.

I smile and murmur again in her ear, "Just wait until I get you home. Won't be no mistaking; Santa's gonna come down the chimney while you're screaming my name."

Violet suddenly shouts from the back seat, "Santa Claus!"

CHAPTER 13

Mary

I register what's happening in front of me.

Along the side of the road is a snowy, reddish shape coming out of a small truck that has skidded and tipped over onto its side. Struggling to extricate himself out through the driver side window is a man in a red suit. And it's a good thing this man in red is not as portly as the Santa Claus we normally think of in the United States' version of Saint Nicholas, but he's still not exactly slim.

"Got room back there for one more, Violet?" Bear says. Bear doesn't seem disturbed in the least by the scene playing out in front of us.

"Baby, if we ain't got room for Santa Claus, we"re all waking up to coal in our stockings," Violet says.

Well, as it turns out, not only can you not leave Santa by the side of the road, you also cannot leave his sack of presents behind.

This time, all of us hop out of the truck to help—all except the person who's just delivered a baby on Christmas Eve.

Rescuing Santa from an overturned truck also feels a little bit like childbirth. The driver side door is stuck, but luckily the old truck had a hand-crank window that allowed him to get himself halfway out.

What happens next is not unlike Rabbit pulling Winnie the Pooh out of his cave. Bear has hold of one arm, Jacob the other, while Violet and Wiseman and I work to help him shimmy out his middle section through the window.

The snowflakes and freezing rain are pelting my face and I can barely see what I'm doing. But eventually we get the fat man out of the truck and safely inside the cab of the tow truck and we're assessing his injuries.

"Thank you everyone," he says, feeling a little sheepish as I'm examining his fingers, his face. Violet is handing over the last available blanket and sweaters to cover him. "But I'm just fine. If you could just drop me off downtown next to the convention center, I'm supposed to make an appearance at the Potter Finance Christmas party tonight. I have a bag full of new game systems for all those kids."

I shake my head, "No way, Santa. We gotta get you to the hospital and get you checked out for frostbite."

Bear grunts out some cuss words about Potter Finance. "I think the slumlords and their kids are already getting plenty of presents from Santa this year," he says.

So, to recap, in the back seat we have baby Mary-Violet, Liz, Jacob, Violet and the sack of toys. In the front seat, Trey Wiseman with a baby camel on his lap, me on Bear's lap, and Santa Claus in the middle. This time, I'm facing the other direction, my back against the window, to make more room for Santa's "man-spread." I'll just say that it's a good thing I'm small. And it's a good thing Santa knows how to drive a stick, or else Bear would have to reach between Santa's knees to shift.

I have never been so happy to see a hospital in my entire life.

Violet has phoned the emergency room and told them we're bringing a fresh new baby and mama to the ER, a camel with PTSD, and a Santa Claus with possible frostbite who was banged up in a car wreck.

Bear's plow clears a path all the way to the doors of the ER, where nurses are waiting in the vestibule with a wheelchair.

Santa also disembarks with his bag of toys and so does Violet, after we help Liz and Jacob out.

"Don't you all want me to bring you home? You'll be stuck here for the night," Bear says.

But Santa and Violet are busily talking to the nursing staff as the OB nurses wheel Liz and baby Mary-Violet away.

Santa comes out and explains that he and Violet are going to stay and pass out some game systems to some very sick kids in the children's wing tonight.

Before she leaves, Violet presses a business card into my palm and winks.

"Just promise me, when you two hotties do get married, let me do the wedding. I not only sing, but I'm an ordained officiant."

"Where you goin'?" Bear asks with a crooked smile when I pile back into his truck and buckle into the passenger side.

I blink at him like he's lost his mind.

"Nowhere. I'm buckling in to the passenger seat, just like my mama taught me to do."

"Fuck that seat belt and get back on my lap," he growls.

I sigh at him.

"Look around you, Bear. There's nobody else in the truck. I don't need to sit on your lap," I say, getting a little exasperated with him.

"You do if I'm gonna get my hands down those pants before I get you home," he says, breathing hard. He's dead serious.

But so am I, about safety.

"Listen, Bear. I'm going to buckle up, and then when we get to your house safely and in one piece, you can do whatever you want to my pants. But I'm not sitting on your lap. I did so out of necessity, but that's it."

Bear throws the truck into gear and peels out back onto the highway. He's driving way too fast for the weather conditions, and I tell him so.

"Dammit, woman, I gotta get you home before my Little Bear rips a hole in my snow pants," he says.

I lean in and trace my hand up his leg. "That'd be a damn shame. Wouldn't want Little Bear getting frost bitten." She peels off her coat and resumes fondling my thigh.

"I can think of a way for you to keep it warm, weather girl," he bites out.

I click my tongue. "While you're driving though?"

"Woman," he says through gritted teeth. "I live for this weather. There is exactly zero chance of you causing an accident."

I slide my hand over his groin and I can feel that rod twitching in response to me. "Then there's no reason you can't just pull over."

He sighs roughly and reaches over to me, resting his palm

on the side of my breast. "Got too many layers on to make that happen in here, baby girl."

He looks over at me and I give him a pout. "Come on, Bear. Where's your Christmas spirit?"

CHAPTER 14

Bear

We are less than a quarter of a mile from my house now.

I can't let her just take the reins. Not when I haven't even properly kissed her yet.

Call me a control freak. But I want to have my way with her first. Need to. Have to.

I let her unbuckle and slide over to me, unzip my coat and unzip the fly in my overalls. She gasps when she sees another layer underneath—long johns.

She's struggling to tug away at all the layers and I can't help but snicker playfully.

"What's so funny?" she asks.

"You really think this is going to play out this way? I can't let you do that when I haven't even tasted those lips yet."

She starts to reply, "But I thought—"

My mouth cuts her off, showing her who's really in control.

At least, that's the plan.

But once I get a taste of her, my control goes right out the window and into a snow drift.

The touch of Mary's velvety lips have me completely undone. They make me feel things I've never felt before. She tastes like candy canes and feels like heated slippers on a cold, ugly morning.

It's all over. She's the one. I found her.

I curse through our joined lips. Mary pulls back and asks me what's wrong.

I cup her face and her eyes are full of self-consciousness. As if anything she could do with that mouth could be wrong.

"Nothing is wrong in my world, weather girl," I say. "I just realized something."

She smiles hesitantly, her eyes glancing between my mouth and my eyes, like she can't wait to get back to kissing me.

"My mom was right about you. She's been telling me to ask you out for ages," I say.

Mary arcs a sultry eyebrow and says, "Always listen to your mother."

Our lips meet again, and my hands are still cupping her chin while hers rest on my thigh. I'm getting hungrier for her, and when my tongue slips past her lips she lets out a little moan. Her fingers grip my thigh tightly. My arms press her close to me. Her hands explore a little higher on my thighs.

Keeping one eye on the road while navigating all these layers of clothing are becoming extremely problematic. My hand smooths around to her sides and up. I caress her breastbone, exposed by the V of her sweater. I feel the goose-flesh there rise to meet me. I take it a little farther and tug at the V, exposing one breast covered in a red satiny bra. Her large breast is close to spilling out of it. The blood rushing to my cock is now headed there at warp speed. At the same time, her hands are peeling back the layers under the zipper of my work overalls and my long johns. She is a determined little thing.

I blaze a trail of warm, slow kisses down her neck and over her exposed collar bone and land my lips at the top of her breast. She is the softest thing I've ever touched and I feel as though I never want to touch anyone or anything else, ever again.

"Got it," she sighs. She's talking about my cock, of course. She's finally struck gold under all those layers of fabric. Mary's grip barely fits around the girth of my shaft. The sensation of her hand around me like that, like she's found herself a precious treasure, sends me through the roof.

"Damn, weather girl. You found the prize."

She smiles. "Oh, is this what Santa brought me for being such a good girl?"

I growl and start to claw the hem of her sweater. She gasps and grips tighter on my rod as I yank down her bra and find her tight little nipple with my mouth. One and then the other. She's gasping softly as I stretch the shit out of her festive little sweater.

"Let it out, weather girl. Nobody's listening now but me."

Mary moans as I rake my teeth and circle my tongue around her nipple as I struggle to keep one eye on the road.

She starts to work over my cock back and forth, and it takes everything in me to keep myself from letting go of my seed right here.

And then, we're in my driveway. I can hardly believe we made it.

I murmur into her neck, "We're home. I need to get you inside. I'm gonna take you. Hold tight."

CHAPTER 15

Mary

Once again he's carrying me like I weigh nothing. He's moving so swiftly I'm afraid he's going to kick down his own front door.

"Bear," I say as he's opening his front door with his foot.

We've left our coats in the truck in our haste. "I need to tell you something."

"You married?"

"No."

He slams the front door behind us. I hardly have time to take in my surroundings before his lips are warm and wet on my cold ones.

"Then it can wait," he says roughly as he sets me down and presses me against the door.

He makes my jeans disappear along with my undies. His breath is hot against my neck.

I reach down between us and dip my hand into his fly again. But this time he stops me.

"Too many layers. I wanna feel all of you. I'm gonna have your sweet pussy wrapped around me all the way down to the hilt."

We furiously fumble with his work overalls. When he's finally got them off, he can't wait any longer to drop his long johns.

"Good enough!" He grits out, hoisting up my legs so I'm wrapped around him and feeling his cock at my opening.

My nails rake over his back. It's not enough. I need to feel his skin against mine.

I yank at his shirt and rub my hands up and down the length of his hard abs.

I'm trying to compel him to take off his shirt but, he grunts out, "You ready? I can't wait another second."

"Let me look at it again," I breathe.

"Fuck," he growls.

I take him in my hand and lightly but surely hold on while I stare at it. Bear's cock is long and thick, and a tempting, urgent shade of red. I rub my thumb over the tip.

He shudders.

I toss aside my sweater that he's stretched all to shit, followed by my bra. He growls at the sight of me.

I take his length in my hands again. I can feel a pearl of pre-cum form on his cock. It coats my finger. I lock my eyes on his while I dab it on my breast.

His breath is like a wild animal now.

"You have a Christmas stocking for that present?" I ask.

He pulls back. "No. And I'm not gonna go find one. You've built up a storm in me, weather girl.

"I didn't need anybody until I found you. And now you belong to me. And that means no raincoat. See, I'm gonna spend the rest of my life with you. Do you understand?"

My breath catches.

Hours ago I would have run screaming from a guy who spoke to me like that.

Right now, all I can see in front of me is a good man.

He sinks his cock partially inside me.

All I see and all I feel is a good man worthy of my love. And my whole life.

"Yes."

He pushes all the way in, and body lights up. I wrap my legs around him, as if having sex up against a door is something I do every day. Everything is easy with him, though.

"Say my name, Mary." His breath and his lips against mine taste and smell like Big Red gum.

"Give me what's mine, Bear. Oh god!" No sooner is his name out of my mouth and he is rearing back and thrusting hard.

He pulls back and thrusts again, this time more wildly, and I rise up farther along the wall with the power of him. "Mary Reed. Do you want to know what I do every night after the weather report?"

His voice is gruff and his charming smile is gone, replaced by a creature consumed by pure lust. His eyes are not a warm fireplace but a raging inferno.

If the length of his beautiful shaft wasn't hitting all the right pleasure points at the moment, I might be afraid of what I'm seeing in those eyes of his.

But I'm not afraid.

Not one moment with him this entire night have I felt anything but safe. Protected. Shielded from the storm.

"What do you do with yourself, Bear?" I ask, playing along even though I already have an idea what the answer is.

He thrusts harder and I cry out as his fingers tighten on my ass.

"I lie in my bed and rub one out, pretending it's your hands on me, or your mouth," he says. "I close my eyes and I see your pretty little tits in whatever tight sweater you were wearing on TV that night. And when I come, I picture myself drenching those tits of yours. And then I fantasize that I'm waking you up with my mouth between your legs the next morning, before driving you to work. You go to work with my cum all over your skin, under your clothes."

I gasp and clench him hard.

"I'm close, weather girl," he says.

"Bear, your fantasy sounds a lot like we're married—" He cuts me off again by devouring my mouth. He really enjoys interrupting me that way, but I don't actually mind.

I moan as he takes one breast into his mouth and suckles it, and then the other.

"Bear…"

"That's because in my fantasy…" he says, punctuating his words with a devastating thrust that has me crying out. He continues, giving one final thrust, "you're already my wife."

CHAPTER 16

Bear

I feel my cum surge into her, filling her completely, just as my movements hit her at the exact spot. She shatters. Her tight sex spasms around me and I'm rocketing into another time and place. I'm so happy I feel like I'm floating.

"Fuck, weather girl," I groan like a wild thing while her orgasm pulls me in deeper and milks me dry.

I pull her in close to me, her tits heaving against my chest as she catches her breath.

I back us away from the wall, but I don't dare put her down.

In fact, my cock is still nestled deep inside as I walk her back to my bedroom.

"It's good you're like carrying me, because I don't think I can walk," she says breathlessly, her eyelashes feathering against my shoulder.

I stroke her hair when we reach the bed. "Did I hurt you?"

She shakes her head and smiles, "Takes more than that to make me sore, cowboy."

And damn if this little sass-mouth isn't making my dick twitch all over again.

60

CHAPTER 17

Mary

I feel like an idiot.

I'm standing here staring at Bear's fireplace, where there are two stockings. One marked "Bear," and the other one, a big, fluffy, cable knit pink one with sequin trim, says "Martha." It's drooping with the weight of presents inside of it.

It's too big to be for a little girl, isn't it?

And surely he would have told me if he had a daughter.

Then it occurs to me he's told me very little about himself.

Could he be…married?

Oh sweet baby Jesus, no.

My hand goes to my mouth. It can't be true. Not after all that talk last night of spending our lives together. It makes no sense.

But the nervous part of my brain reminds me that I'm not

all that great at dating. I might not be very good at catching a liar.

Him being married explains why he was so hesitant to talk about his love life last night.

It explains why I know so little about him.

If he's married, that means I've done it on the bed of another woman. It means I've showered in her shower, dressed myself in her man's boxers and oversized flannel shirt. One she probably folded herself. I'm holding a huge Santa Claus mug of her coffee.

Whoever Martha is, I've done her wrong.

And I realize I couldn't know, but I didn't really probe him for facts about his personal life, did I? I accepted it at face value when he said he wasn't married. I didn't bother with any follow up, did I? No, I'm as much to blame as he is.

I want to run, I want to duck out of there and never see him again.

But my car, obviously, is still stuck somewhere along the highway. I peek outside. The storm has abated but the roads are still impassable.

I text Jenna: *I'm in a bit of a pickle. I can't be sure but I'm starting to wonder if he's married. I'm sure he's not, but I need to find out for sure. And I'm stuck at his house. I'm going to see if there are any other trucks in town that can pull my car out. Or if any cabs are running. Quite a Christmas morning I'm having. Merry Christmas, by the way.*

The reply comes seconds later: *Merry Christmas! Turn on the news!*

I find it odd that she had no response to my new suspicions about Bear, but I turn on the news anyway because, well, she's not just my friend but also still my boss.

I turn on the TV and find Channel 2.

The first thing I see is a shot of my car being pulled out of the snow drift along the highway. And the truck that's pulling it out is none other than Bear Bailey's Snow Angel.

The shot cuts to Jenna, who is holding a microphone and standing next to Bear.

"Jenna! What the hell are you doing on TV?" I shout, even though I'm the only one in the room.

The news editor has not worked in front of a camera in about ten years, but she's still got it. This must be on a time delay or there is no way she would have been texting me a minute ago.

Jenna is speaking into the camera while Bear is looking a bit perplexed and embarrassed. "I'm here with Bear Bailey of Bear Bailey towing, who I'm told spent his entire Christmas Eve night during the weather event rescuing stranded drivers all over the city. Bear, tell us why you decided to do this."

She shoves the mic in Bear's face. He raises his eyebrows as if he hadn't anticipated having to speak on camera. He smiles crookedly and I see the cute little dimple and the sweet, slightly crooked front tooth. He shrugs and his cheeks are flushed. "It's Christmas, and it's just something you do."

And then I know the truth He's not married. He's not a liar. And I didn't wrong anyone. Those eyes, even through the TV, reveal nothing but a pure heart. Martha is somebody, but it's not a wife or girlfriend.

Jenna then asks him a few more questions, they show some more footage, and they even cut to a bedside interview with Liz holding her baby at the hospital. There are about half a dozen people singing Bear's praises.

My heart explodes. I'm so proud to know this man.

Seeing him through the eyes of all the people he's helped just seals the deal in stone. I'm going to marry the best man in town.

The camera cuts back to Jenna. "Well, that's quite a story,

Mr. Bailey. Is there anyone out there you would like to wish a special Merry Christmas to?"

He looks down shyly and a sweet smile spreads across his face and crinkles his eyes at Jenna. "Yeah. I'd like to say Merry Christmas to my mom, and also to my favorite weather girl, Chief Meteorologist Mary Reed." He then turns to the camera. "Mary if you're watching, I love you. And not in a TV fanboy kind of way."

Jenna pulls back the mic and signs off with, "Don't we all just love her? Back to you in the studio, Corky."

I click off the TV and drop the remote. I also drop my phone and cover my mouth.

Just then, I hear keys in the door.

Seconds later the door opens and it's Bear. And also, a huge, floppy-eared yellow lab bounds in out of the snow to greet me.

"Mary, meet Martha," Bear says, and I start to laugh with tears in my eyes.

Martha the dog runs up to me and sniffs, lets me pet her, and then she trots off.

"I didn't see a dog bed, or toys…" I start.

Bear has himself stripped down to his shirt and jeans, kicking off his snow gear in the tile entryway. He greets me with a giant bear hug and his lips are cold when he covers my mouth with his.

"You're freezing," I say.

"Then warm me up," he says gruffly, although he can't hide his smile.

My feet are dangling as he's still got me caught up in his arms.

"I made coffee," I reply.

But instead he rakes the tips of his fingers under the hem of the boxers I'm wearing, which are huge on me. He easily finds my warm folds, which are aroused and damp just at the sight of him.

"I have a better idea," he says.

He plunges a finger inside me and I suck in my breath.

This is going to be the nicest Christmas Day ever.

CHAPTER 18

Bear

She gasps as I find her clit and circle it with my fingers.

I ran you a hot bath," she says.

"Is that so?"

She nods. "I thought your muscles would be tired and achy after all that work this morning."

I run a thumb across her lips and then down her throat, then hook my thumb over the first button on the shirt of mine that she's wearing.

"Wearing my shirt, my boxers. Making coffee. Offering me a bath. Feels like what married people do for each other."

I use that finger to pull her in for a long, deep, smoldering kiss. It's the kind of kiss meant to make a girl feel like she's the only other person on the planet. The kind of kiss meant to make her knees buckle under her. The kind that comes from a man who wants to give her everything and expects nothing in return.

But I do want something.

She must be a mind-reader, because while I'm massaging her sweet, sticky folds with one hand and cupping her breast with the other, she manages to give me exactly what I want.

"I saw you on TV a minute ago. I love you, too, Bear Bailey. And not in a TV fangirl kind of way," she says.

My heart tightens in my chest with love for this woman.

Just 16 hours ago I was fantasizing about this, and now I'm carrying her half-naked body to my tub.

I set her on her feet. She watches me go slow as I strip down, letting her eyes linger over me.

I pull something out of the pocket of my jeans when she turns to light a candle, and I make sure she doesn't see it as I place it on the other side of the tub.

I sink into the hot water, and the Epsom salts feel good. The woman knows how to take care of me, I'll give her that.

Mary sits on the edge and starts to massage my back when I take her hand.

"Spread for me," I command. And she does.

She scoots forward on the edge of the tub so her legs are in the water. Her glistening pink pussy is soaked for me. And I'm thirsty for her.

I take a taste of her and she's like pure, raw honey on my tongue. I run my tongue up and down her smooth folds while she lets out a moan.

"Hold on to the towel rod, baby, I'm just getting started," I instruct her.

My lips find her clit. It's already a hard little stone, ready to allow me to bring her over the edge, and I tease it even more by stroking it with my teeth, my tongue and then my teeth again.

The alternating sensations send her legs trembling.

I pull back then. "Mary, do you trust me?"

She's breathless as she pants out, "Yes, of course I trust you, Bear."

I share her taste with her lips, and she takes it lovingly. "Then I want you to finish while I watch."

"Anything," she moans, reaching her hand down between her legs. The immediate eagerness of this woman is nearly sending me overboard with my own orgasm.

"With this," I say, reaching over the side of the tub and producing a small, purple, silicone object.

Her eyes focus on what I'm holding. "My vibrator?"

"Baby," I say. "I've been thinking about it since I found it in your emergency kit last night. I've been thinking about watching you with it. Will you do that for me?"

A smile creeps across her face. "And here I thought all you thought about was rescuing the helpless on Christmas Eve."

But she doesn't tease me anymore. She does what I ask without a shadow of self-doubt.

And later, I'll do anything she wants. Every day. For the rest of my life.

I've got a 50-year outlook right now, and it's a 100 percent chance of sunshine.

EPILOGUE

One year later

MARY

Bear had wanted a short engagement.

After proposing to me in the bathtub that Christmas morning with a family heirloom ring, he had it in his mind that we should hit the courthouse the very next day.

But as soon as I texted Jenna the good news, she was already planning a date to pick out a dress and a cake.

"We're going to keep it small. Maybe even a quickie, private ceremony," I had told her when we were all back at work a few days later.

She simply blinked at me. "You do know the entire news-room and the crew will want to be there, right? After everything you do for them, they all owe you about 500 wedding gifts, by my count."

When I had told Violet the good news, all bets were off. Not only was Violet going to officiate the ceremony, she also offered the Soda Jerk, with its elaborate stage and large dance floor, as a venue.

Before I could protest, Jenna and Violet were putting their heads together as planner and coordinator. Don't even ask me which of them was the planner and which one of them was the coordinator. The pair became thick as thieves, carrying around binders with fabric swatches, pictures of floral arrangements, and who knows what else.

There was no stopping that train.

Although I wanted to be married to my big Bear as soon as possible, I have to admit it felt nice to let friends plan my wedding for me. I have no clue about dresses or flowers. The only detail I really cared about was the cake. When I finally caved in and gave Jenna and Violet my blessing to proceed with whatever they wanted to cook up, the cake was my only demand.

"Coconut lime cake, because it was my mom's favorite," I said, "and I want snowflake decorations, to honor how Bear and I met."

Cake is really the highlight of a wedding in my book. "Everything else? Meh, go sick," I told them.

I had to break the news to Bear the gentlest way I could.

While I was naked. In bed. With a surprise.

He was muttering in frustration as he came in the door from work.

"Bad day?" I asked, shamelessly spreading my legs for him.

He stopped short when he saw me. A saucy grin slowly spread across his face. "You know what? I don't remember."

As my big Bear undressed and got ready to shower, I said, "don't. I want you dirty, and right now."

Damn if he didn't have a mile long hard-on stretching to be free of his boxer briefs when I said that.

My golden-eyed boy nestled himself between my legs and

hovered over me. His warmth and the scent of hard work was intoxicating. It took so little from him — that look, that scent, the salty taste of him after work — to get my lady bits pulsing with need.

"Wait a minute," he said, stopping short. "What are you up to?"

Damn. So close.

I cleared my throat. "I met with Jenna and Violet today."

Bear narrowed his eyes at me. "What did you do, weather girl?"

I faked offense at his assumption of my motives, which he saw right through. "I didn't do anything. Not exactly."

He sighed and sat up on his knees. "Spill it."

I shrugged. "You know, according to some people, a year is a relatively short engagement."

My Bear looked thoughtful for a moment, and then leaned over me again. I like him just like that: wedged between my legs, his big, sinewy arms caging me in as he hovers, staring down at my face.

He surprised me by softly asking, "You want a real wedding? Dress? Cake? Flowers? The works?"

I smiled. "I want everyone who wants to be there, to be there. And mostly, I want cake."

He laughed. "What my weather girl wants, my weather girl gets. If you're happy, I'm happy."

I pouted. "But I was all set to distract you from being upset. I even got a new toy."

His eyes perked up. "Really? Out with it."

I reached over to the bedside table and show him the fuzzy handcuffs. "I thought I'd been naughty, so I was going to let you punish me."

He didn't laugh.

Instead, he cuffed me to the headboard.

"That doesn't mean we can't use these. If you want a long

engagement, then it just means I get to take my time giving you everything."

The things he did to my body that night make me blush to this day, and we've done plenty of exciting things in the bedroom since then. More importantly, what he does to my soul…every day…makes me light up from within.

And now, it's our wedding day, and it feels like time has flown by.

The year-long engagement has allowed Bear and I to really get to know each other.

Everyone from the TV station is there, as well as everyone we met on the road that fateful Christmas Eve night. Even the camel, and little Mary-Violet.

Jenna and Violet have outdone themselves.

The New Year's Eve wedding night is a riot of snowflake decorations, candles, glittering white lights, and red poinsettias.

The dress that Jenna has picked out for me hugs me in all the right places, especially at my hips. The plunging open back makes me nervous, but, as Jenna says, "I've seen the way he looks at your ass. You're wearing this dress."

Violet, of course, steals the show in a majestic Dolly Parton costume. I had let it slip that Dolly was my favorite singer, and there was no walking Violet back from that decision.

Everything is perfect, but the only things I really care about — Bear and the cake — are beyond perfect.

When Violet declares us husband and wife, Bear scoops me up, much like he did a year before, on the night we met. Everyone cheers and claps as he kisses me deeply, passionately on the mouth.

But instead of putting me down, he starts walking us down the aisle, just like that. "Where are you taking me?"

"I've waited long enough to call you my wife, now we're going to go mark the moment," he growls.

Bear carries me all the way backstage to one of the prop rooms, and locks the door behind us.

"Not up against the door again," I say, but actually not caring how this plays out. His urgency has me wet and ready.

"No. Here," he says, nodding to a large, ornate throne that must have been used in some kind of big, elaborate burlesque number.

I scoff. "We can't do it on Violet's throne! After everything she's done for us, that's so disrespectful."

He rumbles, "Trust me, baby."

"What other choice do I have?" I ask, teasing.

My Bear sits down on the throne, spins me around so I'm sitting on his lap, my back to him. I'm about to ask the question, but he's already answering it with his hands and his mouth.

His lips and tongue are urgently ravaging my bare back. His hands are sliding underneath the fabric of my dress, reaching around to the front, cupping my breasts. My nipples ache for his touch inside the corset that contains them.

"Baby, it's too much work to take all of these undergarments off, just to put them back on again in time to cut the cake."

He grunts, "We can skip the cake and go home."

I grab his wrists, "What did you just say to me?"

He's growling now. "Babe, if you want that damn cake you'd better figure out a way for me to make you pregnant right this second."

I moan at the commanding tone. I like it when he's bossy.

Knowing that he's going to do wicked things to me in my wedding dress is getting me even hotter, and I'm starting to worry about soaking right through the chiffon. My body trembling in anticipation, I stand up and hike the hemline, gathering all the fabric up to my waist.

"Holy shit, I don't know what you call that but … holy shit that's hot," he says.

I giggle. "Garter belts."

His voice becomes suddenly deeper and huskier. "As long as I can still do this." With that, he's got the lace thong pulled to the side and his fingers are stroking my folds.

I cry out in surprise. I spread for him, allowing him to coat his fingers fully in my essence. I have to bite my lip so I don't shout when he finds my clit and works it in erotic circles. He then lets go.

The sound of him unzipping his suit pants has me about to finish immediately. My body knows what's coming next, even though we've never done it this way before.

He pulls me backward; Little Bear — which is not little by any stretch — is pressing against the back of my thigh.

"Take a seat, wife," he says.

I gently do as he says, while he adjusts his position under me and slides the length of him deep inside. This totally new sensation, from this position, is not what I expected. I like to face him, to kiss his mouth while he has his way with my body. But feeling his strong chest against my bare back, one of his hands inside the front of my dress, and the other hand reaching around to pleasure my clit, has me feeling safe. Protected. Warm all over. Add to that the full length of his cock burying into my sex, and I might detonate around him way too soon.

My Bear is so caring, even when he's urgent. And so crafty. Taking me like this, he knows I can only do so much with my hands except hang on tight. He's holding me so close I can't even control the thrusting.

When I feel him gush into me, he hits my hardest-to-reach spot. I come so hard and so rough I forget where I am and I scream out his name. I don't even care if my dress ends up torn to shreds from our love. He's so fully sheathed into me that my body takes in every last drop.

He keeps hold of me as I shudder through my climax, his lips tenderly dotting my bare back with soft kisses.

Bear's hand is still inside the front of my dress, and when he squeezes one breast, I wince a little.

He stiffens under me. "Baby, you all right?"

I smile as I lean back against him and turn my head. "I'm fine. My breasts are a little tender today."

"I'm taking you to the doctor tomorrow. I don't like the sound of that," he says.

I laugh. "I've already been to the doctor, and they say the tenderness might calm down during my second trimester."

I don't know how Bear does it, but he manages the strength to spin me around on his lap to face me. "Trimester? You're pregnant?"

I can't speak without a lump forming in my throat, so I nod.

Bear cups my face and kisses me deeply, slowly, almost worshipfully. He rests his forehead on mine. "Martha's gonna be so jealous," he laughs.

"Nah, she'll be a great big sister. She'll just have to get used to someone getting more presents than her at Christmas."

We laugh as we talk and hug and kiss and plan, almost unaware that there's a room full of people waiting on us to kick off the celebration.

As far as we're concerned, our entire life is going to be a celebration of our love.

"I'm not in any particular rush to let go of this moment," I say. "But I am getting hungry."

Bear grins, full of mischief, when he says, "Maybe if we stay here long enough, someone will bring us some cake."